FROM CRADLE to Sunrise.

ECHOES OF THE SOUL'S FIRST LIGHT

MUKESH SINGH KUSHWAHA

BlueRose ONE .com
Stories Matter
NewDelhi • London

BLUEROSE PUBLISHERS
India | U.K.

BlueRose ONE
Stories Matter
NewDelhi • London

For permissions requests or inquiries regarding this publication, please contact:

BLUEROSE PUBLISHERS
www.BlueRoseONE.com
info@bluerosepublishers.com
+91 8882 898 898
+4407342408967

ISBN: 978-93-7139-948-7

Cover design: Yash Singhal
Typesetting: Namrata Saini

First Edition: September 2025

Contents

Coincidental Perfect Wife

I saw a standing woman in the crowded bus,
Where people were rubbing their shoulders each other.
I requested a gentleman to offer his seat to her,
She did not object and sat like a sincere person there.
I observed that she was exceptionally full of splendor,
Her beauty and charm made my heart tremor.
Her black hair was smooth and longer,
Her blue eyes were captivating me like charmer.
Her nose was long like that of a sniper,
Her glossy lips appearing like sharp scissors.
Her delicate throat was strait and slender,
Her shoulders were broader and stronger.
Her waist was thin and she was taller,
Her body was well-built and she was like beguiler.
Her innocent face was unmatched in looks which was cuter,
Her extraordinary personality was making me perspire.
I was lost thinking about her lusty figure,
She interrupted me by handing over a piece of paper.
I got excited thinking that it might be her number or a love letter,
All my desires and imaginations were hampered.
She asked for my address because she could not hear,
I thought about her, and then thought a little longer.
I proposed to her to marry her in the future,
Her eyes were wet and full of moisture.
She is my wife now and my dedicated lover,
I find myself luckier and happier.

Lesson for Life

Oh! My princess, come to me, closer!
Be good and smart, listener and learner!
Let me tell you a fact, bitter and more bitter!
No success will test you, without making you swelter!
No learning will be permanent, without any failure!
Your knowledge will make you, clever or loafer!
Your good Karma will give you, immense satisfaction and pleasures!
Your kind intention will get you, blessings and well-wishers!
You can't survive in peace, without becoming tougher!
You can't help the poor, without becoming richer!
No one will respect you, without wealth and power!
Now up to you, to be successful or a looser!

Wishlist for My Daughter

Oh, my dear daughter!
Come to me, very closer.
I want you to see higher!
Fly like a bird without fear.
Roam free like a wonder!
Win everything like conqueror!
Always acknowledge your admirer!
Be for nice people, nicer.
Be for tough people, tougher!
Be for kindhearted, kinder!
Become cleaver for the attacker!
Become clever not loafer.

Let's Love Our Nation

Let us make great again, our beloved nation.
Let us not choose, a corrupt and anti-national politician.
Let us have respect, for all ethnicities and religion.
Let us celebrate the diversity, without making any discriminations.
Let us embrace our values, without anybody else assertion.
Let us not incite anyone, based on bandwagon provocation.
Let us contribute something, for the national building mission.
Let us buy Indian products, to support our own industrialization.
Let us boycott all, who promote anti-India ambition.
Let us make strong nation; so, we do not need migration.

I Want to See My Nation High

I wish to see great again, my own nation,
Loving our culture, without embracing half-naked fashion.
Where all the festivals are celebrated, without any discrimination,
Where everybody has wealth and prosperity, beggar-free are all junctions.
All are educated liberally, without undermining our values and tradition.
All may live in peace, without any fear or apprehension.
All may contribute, in the nation-building mission.
Nation pride is supreme, above any faith and religion.
Where all anti-nationals are punished, and the patriots get appreciation.
There is a strong armed-force, capable to defend against any enemy aggression.
All the industries flourish, without any environmental degradation.
Indians must be best, best amongst any civilization.

Princess of a Miserable Father

I have been pushed once again,
To bear life-long pain.
My unending misery I can't contain,
God knows when will be the time to break this chain.
It is becoming difficult to sustain,
All my efforts are going to vain.
When will go away my bane,
I have lost everything without any gain.
I am ready to suffer alone,
Why should the innocent bath under acid rain?
I, moron, do have a nonsense brain,
Why did I drag baby into this polluted domain?
I had all the time to abstain,
My father-feeling couldn't let me refrain.
I must be brought court to arraign,
My desire got a blooming bud to stain.
The baby who is entitled to fame,
She has got nothing except my cocaine.
She has all right to complain,
Her ambition might get slain.
May God give her strength and power to regain,
I wish all the deserving she attain.
All good luck in the world she may retain,
A charm and smile always she may maintain.
She may get an everyday reason for champagne,
No one may match her success of spectacular hurricane.
All health and wealth with her may remain,
All the evil in the world from her may restrain.

Don't Let Others Define You

My excitement is gone now, and has frozen my mind,
I was left yet again all behind.
All my friends have got high-success,
I was stuck in family to grind.
I was crushed into pieces,
The fragmented pieces became impossible to bind.
I became good for nothing,
Lost all my charm and demand.
Not long ago I was amongst the brightest,
Now I am split into pieces to find.
Nobody wants to eat a poisonous fruit,
I am being thrown like useless rind.
I was wishing to die,
An angel came inviting to dine.
She was charming and kind,
She introduced me to the new mankind.
I got ready for the new journey,
I was no longer left blind.
I was not regretting of pined,
Rather cherished everything whatever was designed.
My life is sown people now exemplary,
I am the same but thinking no more confined.
This useless person has become a celebrity,
Everyone wants to follow this expensive brand.

The Days will Come

My life is almost gone,
Waiting for her response.
I failed to understand,
What is behind her no-response.
I am not dejected yet,
She would have rejected in advance.
My hope is not broken apart,
I'm eagerly waiting for my chance.
The day definitely will come,
When together we will dance.
Finally, her compulsion will get over,
We will meet to romance.
We will declare for each other,
All the obstacle will ensconce.
Nothing we will have to complain,
We both will be lost in nonce.
Burning desire for year will flame,
Passionate love making will happen nonchalance.
We will build our new world,
Rejuvenation will be our renaissance.

Lonely Night

I kept you missing all night,
Tossing and terming under moon light.
Nothing has to conceal me,
My bare hand on my looted heart....
Since then, what new took place,
Except that you are not with me today.
My purpose of life is same,
Why have I lost the way?
Was tiresome under open sky,
Lying down with tearful eyes.
A stroke of cold breeze came,
Asking me to not cry.
Those days are now gone by,
But I find myself for you as a stand by.
Have I gotten addicted to you?
May this love go away when I die.

Lost Happiness

How awesome and comfortable life was in those days!
Was not bothering of anything at slightest!
People were innocent without branded clothes and make-up,
Their natural smile and beauty were still the brightest.
Nothing had to do with any double faces,
Quality of life was at its highest.
We always enjoyed and shared life together,
Never pooling-up legs each other to become amongst greatest.
Celebrating festival with the family in a village,
That fun has become impossible and flattest.
Nobody knows where that leisure life has gone,
Is it lost in the survival of the fittest?
Cursing, complaining always about others,
Have I become habitual at latest?

Dear Daughter

You are my life,
I want to see you high.
Have faith in yourself,
You will touch one day, the sky.
Do you know what you are?
You are a clouded future star.
Don't rest until have rest,
Will be surrounded soon by stars.
You are not just gorgeous,
You are more than precious.
Maintain a smile as you do,
Never let effect presents with previous.
You are my hope of life,
Without you, I can't survive.
Never change yourself for somebody else,
Love you ever, as you are.

Life without Her

A round of clock waiting for her phone call,
Staring relentlessly at the book trying to recall.
How and what she must be doing?
Must be missing me, says my soul.
A year ago, how pleasant those times were,
Now I'm broken-up and lost in gall.
I am shivering in this freezing cold night,
Snowfalls are sounding to me like her foot fall.
These chilling winds are absolutely horrifying me,
Something unknown is keeping me alive at all.
Loneliness now is engulfing me without her,
This intense icy wind is making inside me a hole.
Under the blanket I tried hard to divert my focus,
Worked nothing and I remain under pall.
Endless hope is keeping me alive,
Not you, I blame myself for this fall.
I will keep loving you till my last breath,
I am still alive because of you, after all.

Lost Identity

How long will I be slavish?
Enough is enough letting myself petty.
Always pushing down myself on knee to make a plea,
Irrespective of self-respect and dignity.
This commitment will land me in desert,
Left with dusty winds and endless misery.
Sucking my wound and drinking tears,
Yet I will be left hungry and thirsty.
Weltering to have own who can console me,
Won't be anybody even to smile at my adversary.
I must revolt against which I don't like,
Otherwise forever I will be lost in agony.

Lust for Love

I don't find you sexy at all,
But I want you always in my arms.
I've seen sexy amongst the sexiest,
But nobody had your charms.
I have seen everywhere bunches of beauty,
But every time it felt unsafe and alarmed.
Their slim body attracted all,
But to me those were useless and not prime.
Those lost in expensive perfume, dresses, and makeup,
All these seem to me always stilted and derms.
I'm fed up with meaningless parties and corrupt mindset,
I feel you as always kind and warm.
You are the luck of my life,
I want you always to hold you firm.

Lucky to Have You

You are neither attractive nor sexy,
But my heart always keeps longing for you.
I tried to examine the possible reasons for this attachment,
There is nothing obvious for this belonging to you.
Every time you appeal me with your melodious sound,
Those songs in mind keep me bonging of you.
Your pure love and submission,
Will always ask me for prolonging to you.
Innocent heart and your mutual understanding,
These let me every single moment thronging to you.

Where are You, Maa?

I am lost, in a cruel world.
Who will now secure me?
I have become corrupt, suspecting all.
Who will now pure me?
Hopeless, demoralized, with shoulders down.
Who will now manure me?
Double faced, misleading monsters everywhere.
Who will now obscure me?
My dirty minds, with artificial smile.
Who will now assure me?
Whether I am happy or sad,
Who will now care for me?
I keep committing mistake after mistake.
Who will now endure me?
Life is pathetic, without you, maa.
Please come and cure me.

Let the Things Be Straight and Simple

I must be happy today,
And no longer is confusion.
Let the life be simple,
And feel nice without elusion.
Let me obvious of my own doing,
Being practical is a clear solution.
The mantra for all problems is,
All action should be without any expectation.
I should realize the strengths instead of the weaknesses,
Otherwise, I will be lost in own confrontation.
Let's enjoy whatever I have,
Let me forget unrealistic desires and ambition.

Lesson of Life

For how long was I sleeping?
That I lost everything without any realization.
All my friends, relatives, and family,
All meant to me in synchronization.
I used them for my own comfort,
Without giving a damn about anybody's emotion.
Did people love or respected me ever?
Was it because of my wealth demonstration?
I had everything whatever I should have,
Lost all my pure elation.
All my energy was wasted in illusion,
Weltering now for somebody owns consolation.

Let's Have A Satisfying Smile

Let's smile at those who use their smile,
Let's not smile because we have to use our smiles.
Let's smile to make others smile,
Let's not smile to condemn somebody else's smile.
Let's not others dictate our pure smile,
Let's smile whenever we love to smile.
Let's smile to have our real smiles,
Let's not smile because we have to smile.
Let's do the work which yield us smile,
Let's say the truth which makes others smile.
Let's do the things which bring others a smile,
Let's oppose what takes away somebody's smile.
Let's embrace what feel your smile,
Let's celebrate smiles to have a bigger smile.

Nobody is God and Nobody is Devil

All norms, laws, and regulation,
Must be broken by me.
Pre-marriage and extra-marital relation,
Must be accepted by me.
Using smiles and crying for relaxation,
Must be appreciated by me.
Murder, dacoit and corruption,
Must be acknowledged by me.
Rape, molestation and exploitation,
Must be supported by me.
Helpless parents and begging children,
Must be ignored by me.
Human emotions, love and affection,
Must be used by me.
Morality and idealism norms and tradition,
Must be crushed by me.
Worshiping god or devil according to our expectation,
Must be embraced by me.
Everything being fair in this double-faced civilization,
Must be followed by me.

My Type

Want beauty but not stilted,
Want feeling but not which has to be hidden,
Want a relation but not which has been adjusted,
Want a smile but not striven,
Want commitment but not materially prompted,
Want respect but not in compulsion,
Want loyalty but not one sided,
Want love but not driven,
Want desire but one which isn't corrupted,
Want a dream but not broken,
Want somebody to love but not to be left disappointed,
Want trust but not one which is free given.

Let's Love the Life

Oh heart, don't be isolated,
It has been enough of being dejected.
Open your eyes and you will find the palace crowded,
Open your mouth and will find people surrounded.
Open your ear and you will listen various kinds of sounded,
Open your arms and you will feel invited.
Open your mind and you will feel delighted.
Open your window and fresh air will be flooded.
Smell the coffee and you will feel excited.
Take a step otherwise you will be stranded.
Enjoy the life otherwise it will be wasted.
Celebrate everything otherwise you will be outdated.

Joy With Life

I will not let my heart cry anymore.
I will not let my dreams horrify me anymore.
I will not let my desire to die anymore.
I will not let my pain be amplified anymore.
I will not let my emotions to dry anymore.
I will not let my ambition to demoralized anymore.
I will not let my smile to falsify anymore.
I will not let my say be nullified anymore.
I will not let my trust to be defied anymore.
I will not let my mind be preoccupied anymore.
I will not let my hand be tied anymore.
I will not let other to my self-respect to buy anymore.
I will not let my knowledge to certify anymore.
I will not let myself to verify anymore.

Love Yourself

My unknown desire pushed me in constant pain,
I kept sucking wounds hoping for a new dawn.
Always defeating obstacle and trying in to fun,
I am always desperate to be a superman clone.
Without learning those all-silly mistakes,
Unending hope left me creeping along.
I cringe and quail looking at the mirror,
Again, realizing yes, I can smile alone.
I must build upon what I have,
To learn that, what took me so long?

Let's Be Aware of Our Doing

My friend, why do you post everything?
To have just few likes, comment on anything?
Apart from fake friends and their likes,
Have you ever got anything?
Overlooking your self-respect!
Always creating a situation of animosity between?
Dividing people based on caste and religion,
Promoting nonsense to draw little attention?
Keep demolishing unity without own satisfaction?
Without caring for people's feeling and emotion?
Please use your logic and smart brain!
Before jumping to any stupid conclusion.
Mistake after mistake, why don't you learn a lesson?
Let's restrain our self from nonsense bandwagon.

I Will Say My Say

I will love natural faces than half-nude-body vulgar.
I will desire virtue than luster.
I will embrace decent than naked hotter.
I will praise simplicity than seen creator.
I will trust generosity than slicker.
I will prefer Indian army over a misleading actor.
I will admire a nationalist over an opportunist secular.
I will support a patriot over an antinational communal gangster.
I will preserve our values over somebody else's culture.
I will say my say now otherwise never.

It's Up to Us What to Choose

Those who listen their brain, feels satisfied.
Those who listen their heart, feels energized.
Those who listen, their conscience, feels electrified.
Those who listen, their family, feel securitized.
Those who listen their friends, feel organized.
Those who listen their experiences, mind remains suffice.
Those who listen, somebody gets compromised,
Those who listen, anybody gets demoralized,
Those who listen, everybody gets pulverized,
Those who listen, nobody gets paralyzed.

I Wish to Have a Little Princess

I have a desire to have a beautiful baby-girl,
To love her always and never hurt her at all,
Wanting to do anything to make her smile,
I will do everything for that sweet doll.
My all tiredness and sorrow will go away when she smiles,
After taking her in my arms I will be no longer dull.
How exciting will be she holding my finger to walk,
I am dying to listen "papa" from her first call.
Committed to run around with her till she sleeps,
How loving will be to watch her faint footfall,
I will play with her whenever she commands to play,
Even allow her to climb over me like fencing wall.
I will keep her always close to my heart,
And never let her to be touched by any gall,
I will give her all happiness she needs,
I will prove myself the best father amongst all.

My Wonderful Childhood

How wonderful was my innocent desire!
Stealing those mangos, and cucumber!
Enjoying sugarcane trying to curb hunger,
Sleeping on the roof at night all summer;
Light, cold, morning air singing in the ear,
The different booming buds with flower,
Cheering birds flying over,
Playing in mud and rain shower;
Swimming and bathing in the flooded river,
Flying kites higher and higher,
Shouting out of joy louder and louder,
Fighting and calling each other a "liar";
Showing friends my attitude and swagger,
Doing silly thing to get some admirers,
Climbing onto grandpa's shoulders like a climber,
Always throwing tantrums to get some favor;
Hiding till late night from my dad's anger,
Making false promises to not repeat things in future,
I keep missing all those pleasures,
Where have you gone, my pure nature?

Commitment for New Year

Let's welcome the New Year,
By forgetting the pain and misery.
Let's gather the strength to be like a seer,
By suppressing our all adversary.
Let's clear from our minds all fear,
By forgiving all, to let go of agony.
Let's challenged own to steer,
By sucking wounds and injury.
Let's erase the bad luck layer,
By revealing all secrets and mysteries.
Let's face crowd to self-cheer.
By acting to bring self-glory.
Let's take our confidence higher,
By moving ahead for life's victory.

Searching for Myself

She is singing and dancing in joy,
And I am left in agony.
She is smiling on her luck,
And I am cursing my destiny.
She is lost in her utmost happiness,
And I am sucking at my wound and injury.
She is sleeping on a bed of roses,
And I am struggling in misery.
She is surrounded by her friend s all the time,
And I am fighting with my own adversary.
She has everyone to cheer,
And I am lost in my own mystery.
She is hurting me in hating me,
And I keep loving her madly.
She has always last laugh over me,
And I am still searching over her heart victory.

Beautiful Heart

How beautiful your heart is!
Giving shelter to all the poor.
How kind your love is!
Taking everybody's misery over.
How strong your mind is!
In any circumstance, it never surrenders.
How flexible your desire is!
Never complaining about failure.
How nice your destiny is!
Always Everything comes your under.
How glorious your life is!
Full of wonder and thunder.

Wish You to Go Higher and Higher

Though we all love your comedian nature,
Wish you never to alter.
Though taking everybody's misery over,
Wish you never to meet failure.
Though climbing the ladder of success,
Wish you never feet to falter.
Though always God is blessing,
Wish you never to face jolter.
Though life is smooth journey yet,
Wish you never to gate halter.
Though luck and fortune are your friends,
Wish you all to come your under.
Though have been inspiring to all.
Wish you to go higher and higher.

We All are Same

Although my eyes saw innocent faces,
But their appearances were full of gloomy.
Although my heart felt their beauty,
But their soul was shady.
Although my nose smelt scented dresses,
But their mind was filthy.
Although my mind noted their simplicity,
But their desires were full of lusty.
Although my sense loved their honesty,
But their behavior was full of flirty.
Although I found them at a disco party,
But their life was full of misery.
Although my soul demands people with purity,
But I realized all of this is contradictory.

Let's Celebrate Everyday Valentine

It was midnight but people were shouting,
Love song and dance on DJ was on.
The couples were hugging, kissing, and loving,
The surrounding was flooded with perfume, and drinking was on.
My forgotten friends were messaging and calling,
After shutting my room, I kept sleeping on.
My sleep was broken by a knock on the door and the doorbell ringing,
They gave me a greeting card with roses and then they were gone.
I kept questioning if I was changed or if I were the same,
The answer was 'Valentine's' which forced them to act on.
Days after days, many nights have gone by,
Messages have been deleted and roses have dried on.
No more celebration and love, just hating and hating.
Everybody has become stranger again apart from the familiar dawn.

Reality to Ending Life

The beautiful woman which always cherished and cheered,
She has shattered and collapsed like cookies.
The blooming bud which flourished in prosperity,
Before maturing were seeped by honeybees.
The lemon which was fresh and full of juice,
Has now been dried and squeezed.
The personality which was ever warm and pleasing,
Has now been cold like ice freeze.
The queen who reigned over thousands of hearts,
Has now been treated like a disease.
The goddess who loved and helped all,
Has now been herself pleading on her knees.
Though finely we all have to die,
Everyone deserves to die in peace.

Please Come Back, Maa

Whenever I hear your name, maa,
Tears roll down from my eyes.
I keep searching for a reason to smile,
But find nothing worth pushing myself to survive.
Your soul must be watching me,
I never want to cry.
Tell me your address,
I will catch you even in the sky.
Come and bless me,
I want to touch the new high.
I have all except you, maa,
Without you, my life is dry.

Let's Keep Ourself in a Clean Bucket

Surrounding influences your humanitarian thinking,
That thinking reflects on your emotional mind.
Your mind decides your social behaviors,
Your behaviors determine your social relation.
The social relation gives you self-identity,
Self-identity provides you with respect and satisfaction,
A satisfied person is always happy.
Only a happy person can make others happy.
Who don't want to be happy?
We all deserve to be happy.
Let's find the reason to be happy,
Let's we all be happy.

My Heart is on Sale

You must be knowing dear,
My heart is on sale.
I will always serve you,
Please you come and avail.
Whether you make it heaven,
Or let it go to hell.
How did I sell myself to you?
You know everything in detail.
You were always behind me,
Why do I now trail?
Whether you make my life,
Or put me into jail.
My hope should never die,
Your booming cat and dog tale.
It must be something beyond your control,
That's why you are so stale.
You are not happy at all,
Your face is in wail.
You will hail my pure love,
One day your sense will prevail.

Shredding the Life's Leaves

Though my conscience was always aware,
I was destroyed in undesirable desire.
I had fueled this entire flame,
Directed it towards myself this fire.
Scar of my KARMA is still visible,
Nothing could cover me, no attire.
Those who were deserted by unscrupulous means,
Could not be reached by any wire.
Shredded long ago whatever I had,
Nothing could take me out from this mire.
Counting my days laying on the bed,
Nothing will save me in this dire.
Now I have left nothing to cherish about,
Yet something unknown has been keeping me alive since prior.
I started licking my wounds in hope of new dawn,
Some miracle will take me away from this quagmire.

A Woman in the Skirt

I met a woman in the bachelor party,
The temperature was twelve but she was in shorts.
Her personality was super-hot and sexy,
She invited me in her resorts.
She might be in her mid-twenties,
She did swim, danced, and played sports.
I was frozen in the cold so icy,
She was running around in a transparent skirt.
I could sense that something was nasty,
Perhaps she needed some emotional support.
I inquired about her hospitality,
She had nothing at all to report.
She took wine and became mentally free,
She then expelled all from her broken heart.

Life Without Near and Dear

I saw something harsh and bitter,
Somebody was laying down lifelessly in an operation-theater,
He was alone and his eyes were full of tears,
Perhaps, he was longing for his family members,
After some time came his brother,
His brother was in a lavish suit, with a bouncer.
I was there because of my mother,
She inquired about other family members,
I replied that they had their own affairs,
His near and dear ones were the richest amongst the billionaire,
My mother cursed his wife, son and sister,
The man was no more after some hour.
The wealthy man's life ended in a failure,
We were expecting at list his son and daughter.
Unfortunately, none of them came there what so ever,
His body was decomposed without his near and dear.

Wishing for a Peaceful Death

Laying down on the hospital bed,
Perhaps, counting the last breath,
Cherishing all the good deeds done,
Regretting about everything missed before death,
No one is near to cry,
What is use of this accumulated wealth?
All emotions and feelings were crushed,
Got success but at the expense of health,
Can't be ignorant about myself anymore,
Bearing isolation is not in my strength,
Will I die soon without any peace?
I wish not to have such last fate.

One-Night Stand

Searched and searched year after year,
Finally got somebody who accepted my proposal,
We met one day and dated for a few hours.
Then made passionate love in a 5-star hotel.
I woke up in the morning but she was not there,
I found only her written note on the table,
"Goodbye and thank you for the awesome knight together",
I was heartbroken at this unexpected disposal.
I was shocked but I dialed her number,
The number was blocked like I was antisocial,
I talked to thousands about her promiscuous behavior,
One-night stand is apparently the new trend in the global.

Ultimate Beauty

I got swooned watching her ultimate beauty,
My lips went dry and I felt extreme thirsty,
She had a perfect figure and was in her mid-twenties,
Her voluptuous size made me absolutely empty.
I got desperate to talk to the girl so pretty,
I got agitated and was sweating plenty,
My imagination soon got dirty,
I found myself hugging her at a party.
A loud car horn brought me back to my sanity,
In a moment, she was lost in the crowded city,
My broken slippers and torn clothes reminded me of my poverty,
I was left there devastated and guilty.

Don't Bother Me Please

"Hello! Yes, who are you man?"
"Though your voice sounds familiar,"
Shocked and devastated, I was left in agony,
Your ignorance and sarcasm had struck me like thunder!
Year after year has been passed away,
Your call is reminding me my forgotten suffer,
Why your melodious voice is choking-up?
Though hearing your sound again giving me thriller.
Why are you wasting your purl of eyes?
Don't waste your tear for a failure!
I have heard about your immense wealth,
Wealthy people don't miss useless crapper!
You are a celebrity with name and fame,
You can buy everything love and lover!
I don't deserve your second of time madam!
Don't bother me please! Goodbye forever!

Laughing with a Baby

My all agitation and rejection were gone,
Listening after a baby's giggling sound.
All my dejection and frustration were gone,
After watching a baby smiling all-around.
All my misery and sorrow were gone,
After jumping with a baby round and round.
All my sadness and tiredness were gone,
After hearing a melodious baby song in the background.
All my gloominess and melancholy were gone,
After playing with a baby in the playground.
All my discomfort and uneasiness were gone,
After jumping with a baby anywhere around.

Skipping from the Brutal in-laws' House

I encountered a lady, midnight in the downtown,
She was coming to me, from the opposite side in a blue nightgown.
She was walking straight, without looking down,
She was quite attractive, with large eyes brown.
I said 'Hello', and she looked at me upside-down,
She said nothing, but her forehead got a frown.
I gestured her, to 'cool down',
I walked to her, and asked there to sit down.
She stretched her legs over a bench, and she lied down,
Her face was burnt down, and her clothes were torn down.
She had a scar on her body, and her confidence was dropped down,
Her feelings were crushed down, and her self-respect was torn down.
I offered her my help, and she broke down,
I kept her head on my shoulder, and she had a meltdown.
I handed over my beer, in once gulp, she drank it down,
She told all her tragic story, under her in-laws' lockdown.

Let's Face the Breakdown

I was rejected and dejected again,
Once again, I was back my home dropdown.
I was demoralized and my shoulders were down,
I looked like an idiot, a clown.
I talked to nobody and I was ready for a meltdown,
Repeating my mistakes had made me frown.
I closed the door and alone I sat down,
Thinking calmly, I got the reason behind my breakdown.
I stood up with new energy and all I noted down,
I promised myself to not let me drown.
No situation will force me to come down,
No difficulty will compel my heart to shut down.
My will power will make me renown in the town,
I will have over my head a deserving, shining crown.

I Have Found a New Lifeline

Years after years have passed away,
The shadow of memory has started lingering.
Praying for you everywhere, all the time,
I have stopped all-together caring.
The extra layer of your misleading make-up,
It has become irritating and disturbing.
Relentlessly following you on social media,
Facebook, Insta and WhatsApp have become boring.
Neither I crave for your conditional love,
Nor do I see your status updates and keep wondering.
Your compromised relation and corrupt mindset,
No longer keeps me hurting or bothering.
My unconditional emotional and financial support,
No longer I desire to keep you offering.